CW01095681

Bethany the Bananacorn

Scan this code to learn a whole heap of fun facts about Bethany!

www.llamahousebooks.com

For Mathilda Richardson

x

 Other Unicorn Island books:

Bethany the Bananacorn

Megan the Mallowcorn

Amy the Applecorn

Tabitha the Toffeecorn

Sienna the Slushicorn

Bella the Bumblecorn (Sept 2023)

SHOP HERE

ISBN: 978-1-913944-32-2

Published by Llama House Children's Books

Across a secret ocean
Through a magic rainbow-wave,
You'll find a very special place
Where friends are true and brave.

Their land is made of star dust
And the power from their horns,
So turn the page and let's begin
Our tale of unicorns...

A MAP OF MUNCH TOWN

Snatchum Castle

To Solar City

THE SOY SEA

SNATCHUM HILL

BETHANY'S STABLE

Samosa Lane

RAINBOW-BERRY JUNGLE

To Animalcorn Kingdom

Bao Bun Beach

Elderflower Lake

Sherbet Street

Lentil Avenue

BUBBLEGUM PARK

Pasta Parade

The Great River of Magic

Gravy River

SUGAR FROST MOUNTAIN

To Green Fields

To Hobbyville

MEET THE STARS OF THE STORY

BETHANY THE BANANACORN

who uses her magic unicorn power to outsmart the hairy Horn Snatcher.

TABITHA THE TOFFEECORN

who is taken to Snatchum Castle and forced to fill a giant pastry crust with toffee sauce.

CHLOE THE CARROTCORN

who faces the horrid Horn Snatcher to rescue her toffeecorn friend.

MEET THE MUNCH TOWN MISCHIEF MAKER

THE HORN SNATCHER

who likes stealing unicorn magic
and filling his hairy tummy with snacks

CONTENTS

Chapter 1   Rainbow-Berry Jungle   1

Chapter 2   An Enormous Footprint   11

Chapter 3   Snatchum Castle   17

Chapter 4   Bethany's Plan   25

Chapter 5   Sticky Feet   33

Chapter 6   Giant Carrots and Monkey-Finks   39

Chapter 7   Banana Milkshakes   51

Chapter 8   A Pair of Slippers   55

A Sneaky Peek at Amy the Applecorn   63

Unicorn Puzzles   77

RAINBOW-BERRY JUNGLE

"This is it," said Bethany, pointing up at the colourful trees. "Rainbow-Berry Jungle, one of the most beautiful parts of Unicorn Island and my favourite place in the whole world."

In summer, Rainbow-Berry Jungle was covered with blossom. The trees were dappled with pink, yellow, purple and red flowers of all shapes and sizes. Their petals fluttered down from the branches like confetti.

Tabitha the Toffeecorn looked up into the jungle canopy and gasped.

"It looks like a giant bouquet!" she exclaimed.

"And it smells sweet like cherries," smiled Chloe the Carrotcorn. "You're so lucky that you get to come here every day, Bethany."

"Well, someone has to feed the monkeys," she said, "and who's better for feeding monkeys than a bananacorn?"

The unicorns giggled. Then Bethany's tummy made a soft tinkling sound and a beautiful rainbow shone out from her hoof. A ripe, yellow banana appeared at the end of it. The delicious fruit hung like a cloud in the air, hovering like a stripeless bumble-bee, until Chloe took hold of it and peeled away the skin.

"Your unicorn magic makes the best bananas, Bethany," she said, her mouth already stuffed full with the yummy fruit. "No wonder the monkeys like you. I've never even *seen* a monkey, let alone been *friends* with one."

"They're a bit timid, that's all," explained Bethany. "But it's not all about the bananas when it comes to monkeys. You could have every banana in the world and they'd still hide from you. Unless you know the special secret, of course."

"There's a special secret?" gaped Chloe. "What is it?"

"If I tell you," replied Bethany, "do you promise never to tell anyone else? We don't want the whole of Rainbow Jungle overrun with unicorns, all trying to make friends with the monkeys."

They nodded keenly, so Bethany leant forward and lowered her voice.

"The one thing monkeys like to do even more than eating bananas," she whispered, "is laugh."

Tabitha snorted and a little fountain of toffee sauce squirted out of her unicorn horn.

"Oh, Bethany," she giggled, "stop pulling our hooves!"

"It's true," Bethany insisted. "The way to gain a monkey's trust is to make him laugh. Why don't you both stand over there behind that bush and I'll prove it to you?"

Chloe and Tabitha did as she asked, and Bethany magicked several big bunches of yellow bananas. She placed them into a pile on the ground and waited.

But no monkeys appeared.

"You see," said Bethany, "it's not all about the bananas when it comes to monkeys. Watch this." She cleared her throat. "Why did the monkey take her banana to the doctors?" she asked loudly. Her voice bounced from tree to tree like a rubber ball. "Because it wasn't *peeling* well!" she finished.

The branches rustled with interest, but Bethany was just warming up.

"How do monkeys get down the stairs?" she asked, calling up into the branches. "They slide down the banana-ster!"

Five long monkey-tails swung down from the flowers as the branches started to shake. A squeaky chuckle sent a shower of petals floating down from the trees and onto Bethany's head.

"And what do you call a monkey with bananas in his ears?" she asked, blasting out one final joke for good measure. "Anything you like, because he can't hear you!"

Suddenly, a whole troop of monkeys tumbled out of the trees!

They landed on the mossy jungle ground, where they rolled around with laughter as Bethany handed out the bananas.

"Hello, you guys," she chuckled, patting the smallest monkey gently on the head. "How are you all doing today? I've brought some friends to meet you. Don't be afraid. They won't hurt you," and she signalled for Tabitha and Chloe to come out from behind the bush.

The monkeys took one look at the new arrivals. Then they shoved the last pieces of fruit into their mouths and clambered back up into the trees, leaving a big pile of banana skins behind them.

"Quick, Chloe," said Bethany, "tell them a joke before they disappear into the jungle."

Now it was Chloe's turn to panic instead of the monkeys'.

"What, *me?*" she gasped. "But I'm rubbish at jokes. Oh, wait, I do know a funny rhyme though....

There once was a monkey called Krum,
Who liked to do tricks on a drum,
He tripped on his tail,
Fell down with a wail,
And now he has quite a sore-"

★✰☆ ₿ ☆✰★

"I don't think we want to hear the end of that rhyme, thanks, Chloe!" Bethany interrupted. "It sounds a bit rude to me."

Chloe's cheeks turned red.

"I was only going to say that he had a sore *thumb*," she muttered.

"You were not," remarked Tabitha.

"It doesn't matter now anyway," said Bethany. "It sounds like the monkeys have gone. Let's go back to my stable and make up some really funny jokes. Then we can come back later and try again, if you like."

"Great idea," replied Tabitha, but as the three friends left Rainbow-Berry Jungle, no-one spotted the two big, yellow eyes that were peering out at them from the shadow of the trees.

AN ENORMOUS FOOTPRINT

The unicorn friends walked along Sherbet Street and past Bubblegum Park towards Bethany's stable, trying to think up some funny jokes along the way.

"I think I've got one," said Chloe. She stopped in front of Bethany. "What did the monkey have at her birthday party?"

"I don't know," replied Bethany, smiling, "what did the monkey have at her birthday party?"

"A clown!" cried Chloe, and the carrotcorn laughed so much her nostrils flared like two flags in the wind.

Bethany frowned.

"Erm, why is that funny?" she asked.

"You're not really asking me why clowns are funny, are you?" Chloe chortled. "Haven't you ever seen a clown before? Megan the Mallowcorn had one at her birthday party last year and it was the funniest thing *ever*," and she laughed some more.

"Yes, but..." Bethany shook her head. "Never mind. I don't think you quite understand how a joke works, Chloe. Perhaps Tabitha has a better one."

She looked over her shoulder, but Tabitha wasn't there.

"Where is she?" frowned Chloe. "I thought she was right behind us."

"Oh, no, perhaps she went the wrong way and got lost in the jungle," Bethany suggested. "We need to go back and look for her."

Galloping as fast as their little unicorn legs could carry them, the two friends ran all the way back to Rainbow-Berry Jungle.

But when they reached the edge of the trees, there was no sign of Tabitha.

Bethany spotted a big footprint next to the banana skins. She called out to Chloe, who trotted over and looked down at the terrible sight.

"It's got six toes," gasped Chloe, "and there's only one creature on Unicorn Island who has six toes."

"*The Horn Snatcher!*" they both cried together.

Bethany shuddered.

"That horrible creature must have snatched Tabitha when we were leaving the jungle. He wants to use her unicorn magic for some kind of mischief, I bet."

"What are we going to do?" asked Chloe. "We'll never find her amongst all these trees."

Bethany noticed something behind the banana skins. It was a long drizzle of toffee sauce.

"We *will* find her," smiled Bethany. "Look, she's left us a trail. Come on, let's follow it and find out where the Horn Snatcher has taken our friend," and with that, the two brave unicorns disappeared into the jungle.

SNATCHUM CASTLE

Bethany and Chloe picked their way through the thick jungle. They followed the sticky trail around brambles, over logs and under the dangling vines of the enormous trees. It was damp but warm here and by the time they reached the other side of Rainbow-Berry Jungle, their cheeks were glowing pink.

In front of them, an ugly mound of mud and weeds rose up from the ground like an enormous mole-hill. Bethany looked up. Perched on top of it like a rotten fungus was the Horn Snatcher's grey and gloomy castle.

"It's Snatchum Castle," she gasped, "and look, the toffee trail leads right up to it."

"But why would the Horn Snatcher want Tabitha's magic toffee power?" scowled Chloe.

"I don't know, but we'd better rescue her quickly, before he locks her up in his dreary old castle for good."

Quietly and carefully, they started their climb.

It was much colder here than it had been in Rainbow-Berry Jungle and the air had a strong smell of rotten eggs about it. The stink caught in the back of Bethany's throat and then, as they drew closer to the castle, a strange sight came into view.

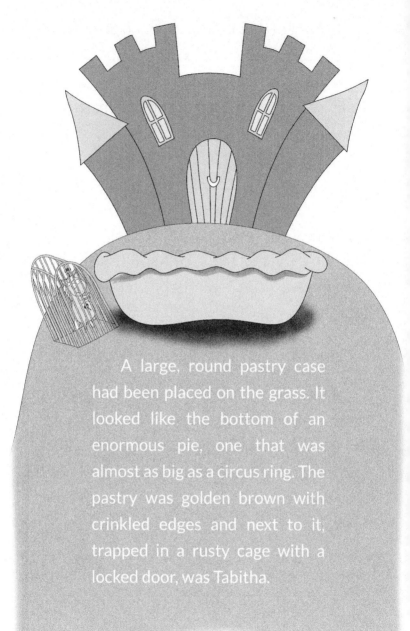

A large, round pastry case had been placed on the grass. It looked like the bottom of an enormous pie, one that was almost as big as a circus ring. The pastry was golden brown with crinkled edges and next to it, trapped in a rusty cage with a locked door, was Tabitha.

"Look what he's making her do!" gasped Chloe, trying to keep her voice low enough so the Horn Snatcher didn't hear.

They hid behind a clump of stinging nettles and watched. With a faint tinkling sound, Tabitha's unicorn magic was squirting a fountain of sweet toffee drizzle from her apple horn. It looked like she was trying to fill up the pastry case with sauce, and there, stepping out of the castle with an enormous grin on his big, hairy face, was....

....THE HORN SNATCHER!

Green fur covered every part of the creature's body. It bristled with excitement as he licked his thin lips with a black tongue.

"Oo, me likes banoffee pie so very muchly!" he sang. "It looks so scrumsy-wumsy that I wants to be scoffing it right now!" He turned to poor Tabitha. "Hurry up, toffeecorn! Me tum-tum's a-rumbling like a hipposaur's botty!"

Bethany and Chloe shuddered.

"You don't think he's going to put *Tabitha* in the pie too, do you, Bethany?"

"No," she replied, "the Horn Snatcher doesn't *eat* unicorns, Chloe - he just likes stealing their magic. Didn't you hear what he said? He's making a banoffee pie."

"What's that?" frowned Chloe.

"It's a dessert made from pastry, toffee and...." Bethany paused, placing a hoof on her magic unicorn symbol as she realised something terrible. "....and *bananas!*"

Chloe gasped.

"Does that mean he'll want to snatch *you* as well?" she sobbed. "I don't want to lose both of my best friends in one day."

"You won't lose anyone," said Bethany. Her eyes narrowed as a tiny rainbow flashed over them. "Listen carefully, Chloe, I have an idea..."

BETHANY'S PLAN

Bethany charged back downhill and fetched the big pile of banana skins from the other side of Rainbow-Berry Jungle. It felt like an endless wait for Chloe, but soon they were both hiding behind the stinging nettles again, ready to put Bethany's plan into action.

"Are you sure you know what to do?" puffed Bethany, still a little out of breath.

"I think so," replied Chloe. "I just hide here with the banana skins until you give the signal. It's lucky the monkeys ate so many bananas earlier on, isn't it?"

"Yes, the more we have, the better our chances of beating that horrid Horn Snatcher. Okay, here I go. Look out for my signal."

"Good luck, Bethany," whispered Chloe. "Be brave."

Taking a deep breath, Bethany stepped out from the nettles and walked towards the giant pastry case.

The Horn Snatcher spotted her at once. He squinted into the sunlight, trying to see the shape of the horn on her head, and a wicked grin swept over his hairy face.

"Is it being Christmas today?" he asked Tabitha.

"Of course not," replied the toffeecorn from inside her rusty cage. "It's ages until Christmas."

"Then why has the bestest present in the whole wide worldsy just come galloping into me garden?" he said.

Tabitha squinted down the hill, took one look at Bethany and gasped.

The Horn Snatcher rubbed his tummy with glee.

"I'm needing some bananas for me scrum-scrum banoffee pie," he cried, "and once I catches that unicorn, I'll have all the bananas I'll be needing forever more. Wahoozy!"

Tabitha stopped magicking toffee sauce and cupped two hooves to her mouth.

"Run, Bethany!" she shouted. He's after your unicorn magic too! Quick, Bethany, run!"

The Horn Snatcher charged towards her.

Bethany felt the breath tremble inside her throat, but she didn't run. She just let the hairy creature move as close as she dared, until she could clearly see the yellow of his eyes. Then she turned tail and quickly galloped back down the hill.

Bethany couldn't see Chloe waiting behind the stinging nettles and neither could the Horn Snatcher, but she headed straight for them. The feet of the greedy creature pounded the muddy ground behind her...

THUMP!
THUMP!
THUMP!

...getting closer with every step, and then...

"Now!" cried Bethany, when she drew level with Chloe's hiding place.

Bethany jumped over the nettles. At the same time, Chloe scooped the banana skins into her arms. Then she stood up and threw them all over the grass.

The skins landed in front of the Horn Snatcher. His yellow eyes bulged from his face like two hard-boiled egg yolks and before he knew what was happening, one of his six-toed feet landed on top of the banana skins. The horrible Horn Snatcher went sliding downhill with a loud, **"AARGH!"**

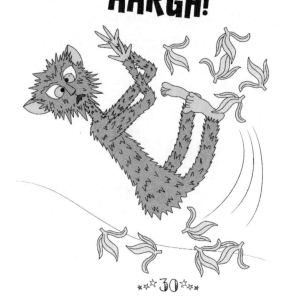

As the creature's voice faded and he disappeared out of sight, Bethany threw her hooves around Chloe's neck and the unicorn friends shared a hug.

"Quickly," said Bethany, "let's rescue Tabitha before he comes back up the hill."

STICKY FEET

Bethany and Chloe ran to the cage.

"The keys are over there by the pastry case," Tabitha said, urgently. "Please be quick though - if the Horn Snatcher comes back, we'll all be in terrible trouble."

As fast as their hooves could carry them, Bethany fetched the key and Chloe unlocked the cage. Tabitha leapt out onto the muddy hill and thanked her friends.

"I'm just glad you're okay," replied Bethany. "I couldn't stand the thought of you being locked in this horrible castle forever with that awful creature." Bethany felt something wet and sticky on her feet. "What on earth....?"

Looking down, the unicorns saw that the toffee had leaked out of the pastry case and drizzled downhill towards Bethany. The sauce had run all over her hooves!

Bethany tried to move, but the sauce was so sticky she couldn't take a single step.

Suddenly, the Horn Snatcher appeared in the distance at the bottom of the hill. He was rocketing towards them like a steam train, huffing and puffing and waving his hairy arms in anger.

"Hold onto my hooves and I'll pull you free!" cried Tabitha.

But no matter how hard she pulled, Bethany's feet remained firmly stuck to the ground.

"Let's both try pulling," suggested Chloe, and the two of them took hold of Bethany and heaved with all their might.

There was a loud....

SCHLUP!

...as Bethany's feet unstuck from the toffee sauce.

The three unicorns went flying backwards, straight through the open door of the cage. They landed in a crumpled heap, then the Horn Snatcher slammed the door closed and turned the key in the lock.

"Yippee doo dah!" he cheered. "I've snaffled me a toffeecorn and a bananacorn, so now I can be having me banoffee pie whenever I is fancying it! Scrum-buckets!"

The three unicorn friends sighed miserably.

"What are we going to do?" asked Tabitha.

"I don't think there's anything we *can* do," replied Bethany.

GIANT CARROTS AND MONKEY-FINKS

The Horn Snatcher danced around the giant pie case with glee, clapping his hands and stomping his enormous feet.

"You'd better be magicking some big bunches of bananas," he sniggered, "because you're staying out here until me scrum-scrum banoffee pie is finished, even if it's taking you *all nightsy!*"

"I don't like the dark," whispered Chloe, "and I bet it's *really* cold up here on this miserable hill."

Bethany scratched her banana horn and suddenly an idea popped into her head. She quickly started magicking bananas into the air above the pastry case.

"What are you doing?" gasped Chloe. "Why are you helping that horrid Horn Snatcher?"

"Chloe's right," said Tabitha. "I should never have filled the pastry case with toffee sauce. I'd rather stay out here in the dark all night than go in that dusty old castle anyway."

"Don't worry," whispered Bethany, "I have a plan." She raised her voice and shouted, "Hey, Horn Snatcher - what fruit do sheep like to eat?"

Chloe and Tabitha looked at each other with wide eyes.

"She's gone potty," muttered Chloe.

"Totally round the bend," agreed Tabitha.

"Shush!" said Bethany. This time, she shouted even louder. "Oi, hair-ball - I said, what fruit do sheep like to eat?"

The creature furrowed its eyebrows into a low scowl.

"I didn't know sheepsies eat fruit at all," he said. "Does they be liking strawbugs?"

"No," replied Bethany, loudly. "Sheep like to eat *baaaaa*-nanas!"

The Horn Snatcher scratched at his head with his long fingers, as Bethany magicked more bananas.

"Erm, Bethany," Chloe said, carefully, "what are you doing?"

But Bethany wasn't listening.

"Hey, fuzz-face," she shouted, "if a man has twenty bananas in one hand and eighteen bananas in the other hand, what does he have?"

"I is no good at the maths thingummies," replied the Horn Snatcher. "It frazzles me brainsy and I never knows the answers. Stop with your weirdsy questions, peskicorn!"

"I'll tell you the answer," grinned Bethany. "If a man has twenty bananas in one hand and eighteen bananas in the other hand, he has...enormous hands!"

A rumble came from the bottom of the hill. It sounded like feet hitting the ground, lots of feet, and it was heading their way. But the Horn Snatcher was too busy staring at all of the bananas Bethany was still magicking to notice.

"What's that noise?" asked Tabitha.

"I'm not sure," replied Chloe. "But it sounds like an elephant with a hundred legs is galloping up Snatchum Hill."

"Crikey," breathed Tabitha, "you don't think it really *is* an elephant with a hundred legs, do you?"

"It's not an elephant," said Bethany. "But it does have a hundred legs. Then she shouted her final joke as loudly as she possibly could. "Oi, bushy-bonce - what kind of keys can open a banana?"

"Stop, stop, stop!" cried the Horn Snatcher, now clutching his ears.

Chloe and Tabitha looked at each other. They'd figured out the answer to Bethany's joke and suddenly knew what was happening.

"Mon-*keys!*" they cried, looking downhill towards the sound of feet, and at that very moment two-hundred monkeys appeared in the distance.

They were thundering uphill like a herd of wildebeests.

The Horn Snatcher looked confused by the noise. He couldn't quite figure out where it was coming from.

Bethany chewed at her hoof.

"If he sees the monkeys too soon," she whispered, "my plan won't work. There's no time to explain, but we need to distract him."

"No problem," smiled Chloe, and with a flash of rainbow light, a huge carrot sprouted up from the ground in front of them.

Chloe reached out through the bars of the cage. She pulled the carrot out of the mud, raised the enormous vegetable over her shoulder and hurled it out of the metal prison.

It soared over the gigantic pie, where it struck the Horn Snatcher smack-bang on the side of his fuzzy head.

"Ouchy!" he cried. He stopped wondering about the noise and instead turned to face the unicorns. "You rotten carrotcorn! You've hurt me noggin and now my brainsy feels like—"

Before the Horn Snatcher could finish his sentence, the monkeys leapt at the bananas, knocking the furry menace right into the sticky banoffee pie with a huge...

...and tipping over the cage with a loud....

CLANG!

The cage door sprung open and the unicorns scrambled free. They watched as the Horn Snatcher tried to pull himself out of the pie, but Tabitha's toffee sauce had made sure he was well and truly stuck.

"You needs to be stopping these monkey-finks from eating me banoffee pie!" he cried, as the monkeys realised it wasn't just *bananas* they liked to eat. "You needs to be unsticking me and helping me out of this pie before there's no scrum-scrum left for the Horn Snatcher's tum-tum."

"Hm," smiled Bethany, "I don't think we will actually. Come on, girls - let's go back to my stable and I'll make us all a nice banana milkshake."

"Come backsy!" wailed the Horn Snatcher. "I am liking banana milky-shakes too, but I am not liking these monkey-finks. If you comes backsy, I will not be stealing any more unicorn magic, I promises. Come backsy, unicorns, come backsy!" but the three friends just galloped off down the hill without looking back.

BANANA MILKSHAKES

"That was *such* a brilliant plan," laughed Tabitha, when the three unicorns were all safe and sound in Bethany's kitchen. "Bananas and jokes were bound to bring your monkey friends to the top of Snatchum Hill, where they could save us from that awful Horn Snatcher."

"Of course, we knew your plan all along," added Chloe.

"Yes," Tabitha quickly agreed. "We didn't *actually* think you were potty or round the bend, Bethany, really we didn't."

Bethany giggled as she magicked some bananas into the mixer. She whizzed it up with some milk and added a scoop of ice-cream.

"It's okay," she replied, "I'm sure it seemed like I'd gone a bit potty, and my plan wouldn't have worked without your quick-thinking, Chloe. That was the biggest carrot I've ever seen! Can you put some toffee drizzle on top of these milkshakes please, Tabitha?"

The toffeecorn squirted some sauce onto the banana milkshakes and the three of them slurped their delicious drinks.

"Oo, scrummy!" exclaimed Tabitha. She sighed. "I do so wish the monkeys weren't frightened of me though. I don't think I'll ever be funny enough to be friends with them."

"Me neither," said Chloe. "I'm just so rubbish at jokes."

On the kitchen counter near the mixer, Bethany noticed the small pile of banana skins. She eyed them carefully for a short moment.

"Actually," she said, "there might be a way you can get the monkeys to trust you without telling any jokes at all."

"But how?" asked Chloe.

"You'll see," answered Bethany. "Now, pass me a needle and thread, and I'll show you what I mean."

A PAIR OF SLIPPERS

Bethany walked ahead of her two friends as they made their way back towards Rainbow-Berry Jungle.

"Are you sure we don't look silly?" asked Tabitha, struggling to keep up.

"Of course not," replied Bethany. "Why on earth would you think you look....

...SILLY?"

"I must say," began Chloe, "you're very good at sewing, Bethany, but this doesn't make any sense at all."

"Yes," agreed Tabitha, scratching her head, "I thought you said it wasn't all about the bananas when it comes to monkeys, so how are two **GIANT BANANAS** going to stop them being afraid of us?"

"Trust me," replied Bethany, "in a few minutes, the monkeys are going to love you." She instructed Chloe and Tabitha to move closer to the trees, so the monkeys could see them properly. "Aren't you going to tell them a joke now?" asked Chloe.

"No," replied Bethany, "you'll make them laugh all by yourselves. Look, here they come!"

A sea of faces appeared in the flowers above them. They blinked down at Tabitha and Chloe, eyeing their banana costumes with interest. Until slowly, one by one, the monkeys began to laugh.

It started out as a soft
chuckle...

...which gradually
turned into shrieks
and whoops...

...until the monkeys
dropped from the
branches like big, fluffy
acorns onto the jungle
ground, where they rolled
around holding their
tummies and pointing at
the two giant bananas in
front of them.

"Hey," scowled Tabitha, "I thought you said we don't look silly."

Bethany couldn't help laughing too.

"Well, maybe you look just a *bit* silly," she admitted, "but monkeys love bananas and monkeys love laughing, so what's better to gain their trust than two giant bananas that make them laugh? They're not frightened now you're wearing a silly costume. Look."

Bethany was right. The monkeys weren't in the least bit scared. In fact, they were leaping around with delight and waving their long monkey-tails with joy.

Tabitha and Chloe beamed with happiness. Then they crouched down to pet the monkeys, who climbed onto their new friends' shoulders as if they were trees. Oh, what a funny sight it was!

"Wait," said Chloe, "I think I've got one."

Bethany frowned.

"Got one of what?" she asked.

"A joke, of course," said Chloe, taking hold of Tabitha's hoof. The two unicorn friends stood next to each other in their funny costumes.

"What do you call two bananas?" asked Chloe, in a loud voice.

The monkeys fell silent and shrugged.

"We don't know," replied Bethany. "What do you call two bananas?"

Chloe started to giggle before giving the answer.

"A pair of slippers!" she cried.

The monkeys thought about that for a moment.

Then suddenly, in a fit of hysterics, they whooped and shrieked and guffawed with laughter. Bethany had never seen them laugh so hard.

"You did it, Chloe," chuckled Tabitha. "You finally told a good joke."

"What's more," added Bethany, "you've made friends with the monkeys and there isn't a banana in sight. Well, no *real* ones anyway."

"It's not all about the bananas when it comes to monkeys, you know, Bethany," winked Chloe, and they all laughed along with their monkey friends, as Bethany the Bananacorn magicked enough ripe, yellow bananas for everyone.

⋆✩☆**The End** ☆✩⋆

Turn the page for a

 **SNEAKY PEEK**

at the next Unicorn Island book, starring:

Amy
the
Applecorn

AMY THE APPLECORN

who magics the world's tallest apple tree to defeat the hairy Horn Snatcher.

CHARLOTTE THE CHILLICORN

who uses her fiery chilli-breath to fly a hot air balloon over Bao Bun Beach.

CHESTER THE CHOCOCORN

who helps Amy carve a rowing-boat from a giant chunk of chocolate.

BAO BUN BEACH

The summer sun warmed the Soy Sea as Amy the Applecorn sat down on Bao Bun Beach. She watched the jelly-sharks play in the waves as the nomnom birds squawked overhead. Then she reached for her cup, took a long sip of her milkshake and sighed happily.

"I love the beach," she smiled, pouring Charlotte the Chillicorn some of the chocolate milk. "On the other side of Unicorn Island, they only have pebbles on their beaches. We're so lucky to have these tasty dumplings instead."

Chester the Chococorn reached for one of the bao buns. He dipped it into a nearby rock-pool, one that was full of delicious sauce from the Soy Sea, and took a huge bite out of it.

"Yum! Bao Bun Beach is the perfect place for a picnic," he said. Chester turned to her chillicorn friend. "Charlotte, please could you warm up my drink and turn it into a hot chocolate?"

Charlotte nodded and then breathed her chilli-breath onto the side of Chester's cup until the liquid was steaming hot.

"I've made us some sandwiches," Charlotte told them, handing each of them a neatly wrapped package. "I was visited yesterday by a nomnom bird who brought me one of her eggs, so I've made us some fiery-egg sandwiches."

Chester gasped.

"You were given an egg by a nomnom bird?" he gaped.

"Wow, Charlotte," added Amy, "you must've done something really special. The nomnom birds hardly ever give their eggs away and they're meant to be the tastiest on the island."

Charlotte's cheeks turned pink.

"Well, I come here once a week to do litter-picking," she told them. "I think they like having a clean beach to live on. Anyway, try your sandwiches - I hope I haven't put too much chilli in them."

Amy and Chester bit eagerly into the bread. The crusts were so soft and the eggs were so tasty, but Charlotte's chilli magic had made them extra-scrummy.

When Chester had finished his sandwich, he clapped his hands together with excitement - he had brought the chocolate milkshakes and Charlotte had made the sandwiches, so now it was Amy's turn to show them the dessert.

Would it be apple cake or apple turnover?

 Perhaps it was apple crumble or apple donuts.

Or maybe she had asked Tabitha the Toffeecorn to help her make toffee apples. Chester couldn't wait to find out!

"What are we having for pudding, Amy?" he asked with eyes like saucers.

The applecorn smiled as a soft tinkling sound came from her tummy. A beautiful rainbow gleamed out from her hoof and three green apples appeared at the end of it. The fruits bobbed on the sea breeze like gulls on the water, as Amy beamed proudly.

But Chester the Chococorn just wrinkled his muzzle.

"Are you going to make a pie with those?" he asked, hopefully.

Amy's face crumpled like an accordion.

"I'm an applecorn," she frowned, "not an apple-*pie*-corn. And anyway, my apples are delicious just the way they are."

"That's true," agreed Chester. "Your magic makes the tastiest apples on the whole island. It's just, I thought we'd be having something a bit more...you know."

Charlotte cringed as Amy sat up like someone had just stuck a pin in her.

"A bit more *what?*" she asked.

The chococorn wriggled awkwardly.

"Well," replied Chester, "a bit more....interesting, I suppose. Oo, I have an idea! Why don't I cover them with chocolate for us?"

"No, thank you," Amy said quickly. "I can make them more interesting myself. If you want apple pie, you can have apple pie."

As Amy spoke, her tummy started to glow again and a rainbow of unicorn magic streamed out from her hoof. She had never magicked an apple pie before and she had no idea what she was doing, but she pointed her magic at the three apples and waited.

The fruits started to tremble, then the skins peeled away and spiralled up into the air. Charlotte and Chester leant forward to watch the strange sight with interest, but all of a sudden....

The apples exploded into a terrible mess. They splattered all over the unicorns' faces and all over Bao Bun Beach.

Chester wiped the juice from his eye with a scowl.

"That's gross!" he exclaimed, flicking a lump of apple from the tip of his ear. "It's all over everywhere!"

"Hey!" cried Amy. "My apples are not gross!"

"I'm sure that's not what she meant," said Charlotte, trying to keep the peace. "Let's just forget about pudding and go for a walk instead."

But Amy and Chester weren't listening.

"Why didn't you just let me put chocolate on them?" asked Chester with annoyance. "Then we wouldn't all be covered in gunk."

"Because I....I *meant* for that to happen," lied Amy. "It's apple mash."

One of the jelly-sharks laughed from its watery home.

"Apple mash?" snorted Chester. "There's no such thing."

"Then how come you have it all over your face?" Amy sniped.

As the two unicorns continued to argue, Charlotte noticed something green floating on the surface of the Soy Sea. It was close to the shore and it looked like seaweed.

Charlotte loved cooking seaweed with chilli, especially after it had been soaking in the Soy Sea for a while, so she got up and went over to investigate.

Amy and Chester were too busy arguing to notice Charlotte walking into the shallow waves. The chillicorn peered closely at the plant. It didn't look like anything she had ever seen in the ocean before. In fact, it looked more like hair then seaweed.

Suddenly, in a soggy explosion of soy sauce and wet fur, a green monster burst out from the waves. It was the Horn Snatcher and he grinned menacingly, his eyes yellow like gone-off custard.

Poor Charlotte squealed, but her cries were drowned out by the sound of Amy and Chester's voices. So the Horn Snatcher picked up the chillicorn, tucked her under his stinky arm-pit and ran off towards the Salt Cliffs.

This was already the worst picnic *ever* and it was about to get much, *much* worse.

FIND OUT WHAT HAPPENS TO AMY, CHESTER AND CHARLOTTE IN THE NEXT UNICORN ISLAND BOOK -

AMY THE APPLECORN

Turn the page for some awesome

✦✧☆ UNICORN PUZZLES ☆✦✧

with:

BETHANY THE BANANACORN

CHLOE THE CARROTCORN

AND

TABITHA THE TOFFEECORN

SPOT THE DIFFERENCE

Can you find 8 differences between these two pictures?

MONKEY MAZE

Can you help Bethany and the monkeys reach the bananas?

Answer on page 93

THE HORN SNATCHER'S WORD-SEARCH

Can you find 10 words in this grid to describe the wicked Horn Snatcher?

S	K	B	Y	T	S	A	N	J	H	M	H	S
F	G	H	N	V	Q	H	W	S	G	O	L	L
S	D	N	K	R	P	H	O	L	E	A	P	Y
U	Q	I	W	S	D	G	H	O	R	R	I	D
E	A	T	J	D	U	H	W	O	P	L	H	T
H	H	W	H	H	D	N	I	K	N	U	F	J
C	C	I	B	I	Z	Q	E	E	F	R	H	H
M	H	T	H	Y	Y	H	D	S	A	E	Y	E
E	H	S	Z	V	L	G	J	Y	D	M	O	C
A	F	H	Q	Z	L	N	M	O	H	F	L	N
N	Y	E	B	G	I	H	U	A	A	M	B	A
F	N	R	P	L	S	B	Y	F	I	E	C	S
H	V	J	W	E	T	P	G	T	R	B	H	I
T	F	H	T	E	Z	D	J	K	Y	H	H	U
H	H	S	N	E	A	K	Y	B	J	O	H	N

HORRID   SNEAKY
MEAN   SLY
HAIRY   NUISANCE
NASTY   NITWIT
SILLY   UNKIND

Answers on page 95

⋆☆ 93 ☆⋆

GRAB THE KEYS

Which string should Chloe pull to rescue Tabitha from the cage?

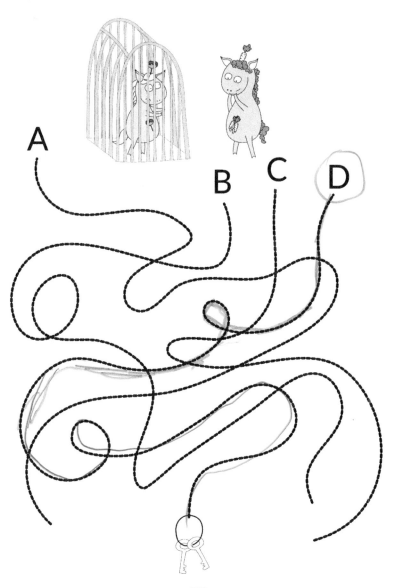

CREATE YOUR OWN MUNCH TOWN UNICORN

Design a new unicorn by choosing a magic symbol.
Add a horn, mane and tail, then colour in your
creation.

My unicorn's name is ....Canpania.......**the**.....Custardcon....

HOW MANY MONKEYS?

How many monkeys can you see in this picture? Put a circle around each of them.

Answer on page 99

SPOT THE DIFFERENCE
ANSWERS

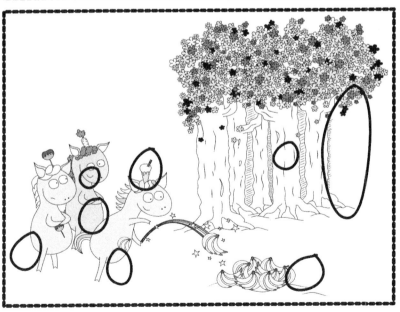

MONKEY MAZE
ANSWER

THE HORN SNATCHER'S WORD-SEARCH

ANSWERS

S	K	B	Y	T	S	A	N	J	H	M	H	$
F	G	H	N	V	Q	H	W	S	G	O	L	L
S	D	N	K	R	P	H	O	L	E	A	P	Y
U	Q	I	W	S	D	G	H	O	R	R	I	D
E	A	T	J	D	U	H	W	O	P	L	H	T
H	H	W	H	H	D	N	I	K	N	U	F	J
C	C	I	B	I	Z	Q	E	E	F	R	H	H
M	H	T	H	Y	Y	H	D	S	A	E	Y	E
E	H	S	Z	V	L	G	J	Y	D	M	O	C
A	F	H	Q	Z	L	N	M	O	H	F	L	N
N	Y	E	B	G	I	H	U	A	A	M	B	A
F	N	R	P	L	S	B	Y	F	I	E	C	S
H	V	J	W	E	T	P	G	T	R	B	H	I
T	F	H	T	E	Z	D	J	K	Y	H	H	U
H	H	S	N	E	A	K	Y	B	J	O	H	N

HORRID   SNEAKY
MEAN   SLY
HAIRY   NUISANCE
NASTY   NITWIT
SILLY   UNKIND

★☆ 105 ☆★

GRAB THE KEYS
ANSWER

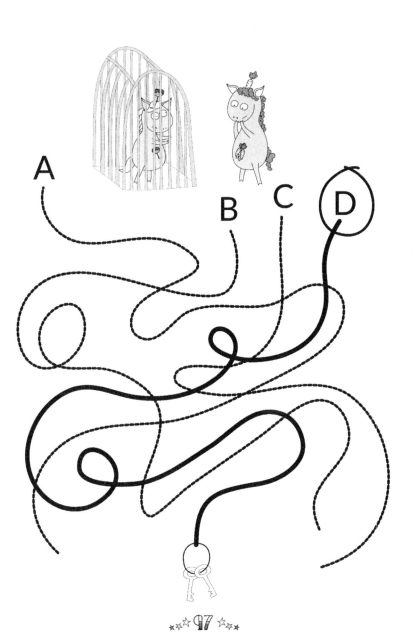

HOW MANY MONKEYS?
ANSWER

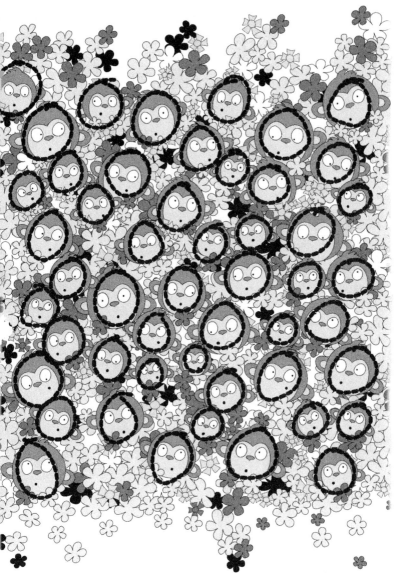

There are **50** monkeys hiding in the flowers.

BOOK SET 1: THE MUNCH TOWN UNICORNS

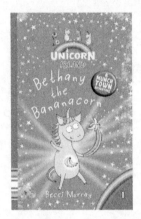

SHOP HERE

COLLECT THEM ALL!

COMING SOON!

BOOK SET 2: THE UNICORNS OF ANIMALCORN KINGDOM

you'll also receive FREE printable Unicorn Island colouring pages when you sign up!

**SUBSCRIBE TO OUR NEWSLETTER
AND BE THE FIRST TO KNOW WHEN BOOK SET 2 IS RELEASED!**

More books from the same author

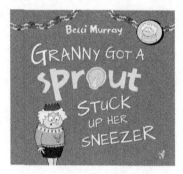

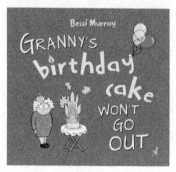

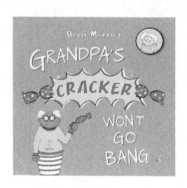

www.llamahousebooks.com

Becci Murray is a mum and proudly independent author from the UK. She used to write for children's television and is the creator of the best-selling 'Granny' book series.

If you enjoyed reading this story, please leave a review wherever you purchased the book to help other young readers discover Unicorn Island.

Thank you so much for supporting an independent author.

www.llamahousebooks.com

Printed in Great Britain
by Amazon

42496051R00066